D0114350

Creative Director: **Susie Garland Rice**
Art Direction and Graphic Design: **Melanie M. Lewallen**

10751a/The Princess & the Pea

A Hans Christian Anderson Story
Adapted by: **Amy Houts**
Illustrations by: **Emily Owens**

Once upon a time there was a prince who traveled many days to distant lands looking for a real princess to marry.

He talked
with beautiful
ladies,
but each
one of them
caused him
to doubt
that she was
a real
princess.

Finally, the prince was exhausted from his travels and returned to his castle feeling very sad. He had not found a suitable wife.

One stormy night, a beautiful young lady knocked at the castle gate. The king himself went to open it, and invited her inside to warm herself by the fire.

"She claims she is a princess," said the king. But the poor princess was dripping wet, and did not look like a princess at all!

The queen hurried to the guest room
and took the pillow, covers, sheets,
even the mattress off the bed.
She placed a single round green pea
in the middle of the bedstead.

"We'll see if this young lady is a real princess," thought the queen.

With the help
of the maid,
the queen stacked
a colorful assortment
of mattresses on
top of the pea.

Some of the mattresses were stuffed with the finest wool from the royal herd of sheep, and some were bursting with the finest feathers from the royal flock of birds.

The stack of mattresses rose so high
that the queen was unable to continue.
So she carefully balanced on the maid's
shoulders until all but one of the
mattresses were in place.

For the final mattress, the maid fetched the royal flock of eider ducks.

The queen and her maid plucked the feathers
of the ducks to fill a drawstring sack
with the finest, softest eider down.

Twenty quilts and blankets of the most luxurious fabric were piled atop the mattresses to keep the princess warm and help her sleep in deep, sweet-dream comfort. The smoothest silks graced the bed, as did plush velvets trimmed with lace, and the warmest furs.

"Your bed is ready," said the queen. The princess climbed the ladder to the top.

In the morning, the queen asked the princess if she had slept well. "No," yawned the princess. "There was something hard in the bed, and after lying on it all night, my whole body is sore."

The queen smiled, because she knew that only a real princess would be so sensitive and so delicate that she could feel a small pea through 20 mattresses. So the prince and princess were married, and there was much joy and celebration in the kingdom.

the Pea

the Princess

The 20 mattresses, 20 blankets, and the pea were placed on display in the royal museum for everyone to view. All agreed that the prince's bride was surely a real princess.

When the prince and princess had their first child, the queen was chosen to prepare the royal cradle.

And they all slept happily ever after.

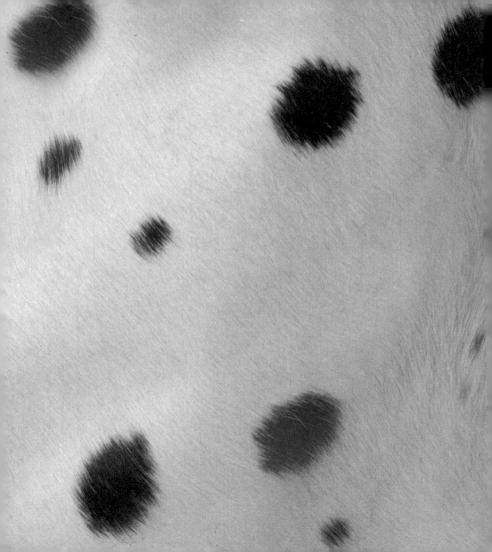